MY CAT

Jonathan Allen

M
MACMILLAN
CHILDREN'S BOOKS

To Wilfred; a wonderful cat, died September 1985.

First published 1986 by
MACMILLAN CHILDREN'S BOOKS
A division of Macmillan Publishers Limited
London and Basingstoke
Associated companies throughout the world

Picturemac edition published 1988

Reprinted 1989

British Library Cataloguing in Publication Data
Allen, Jonathan, 1957 -
    My cat.—(Picturemac).
    I. Title
    823'.914[J]   PZ7
ISBN 0-333-46259-9

Printed in Hong Kong

There are lots of different cats in the world,
but my cat is a tabby cat.

We got my cat when she was very little.
My friend Leroy's cat had kittens,
and his mum said I could have one.

Kittens are fun - they play all the time.

They've got sharp claws though!

Now she's a grown-up cat she
spends most of her time sleeping,
and likes to find the most comfortable places.

She likes soft cushions, and being warm.

She likes to sit on my lap and purr.

She likes being stroked and tickled under her chin;
she shuts her eyes when I do this.

When I get up, she goes to
the warm patch I left behind.

My cat is very fond of food
and meows to let us know when she's hungry.

She rubs round my legs when I open the tin.

She also meows when she wants to go outside.

In the garden, she likes to sit in the sun
and watch the birds on the bird table.
She wishes she could catch them.
Sometimes she tries to.

Sometimes she feels playful and pretends
to catch a feather that I give her.

When she catches it she rolls over,
just like she did when she was a kitten.

She's a very clean cat, and she often washes herself
with her tongue and paws.

Then she sometimes sharpens her claws on the furniture.

She's not allowed to do this.

We always put her out at night.

She meets other cats in the garden.
Sometimes they are her friends,
sometimes they are not.

When the cat she meets isn't a friend
she hisses at it and tries to make herself
look as big and frightening as possible.

I get a bit worried when I hear cats fighting in the night,
but my cat is always perfectly all right
when I let her in in the morning.

I like my cat.